MODEL № 26

the PERUVIAN
double-winged SPITFIRE

a SOUTH AMERICAN Aviation wonder..
Watch your Hats!

STEPS:

① Start here
② Do this
③ then this
④ and this
⑤ Do these things
⑥ and Finish Here.

①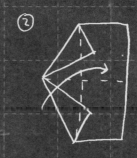

②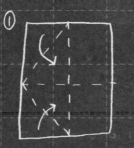

③

④

⑤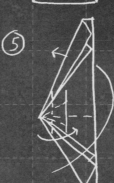

⑥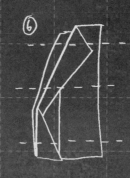

THROWING SUGGESTIONS:

use your left arm.

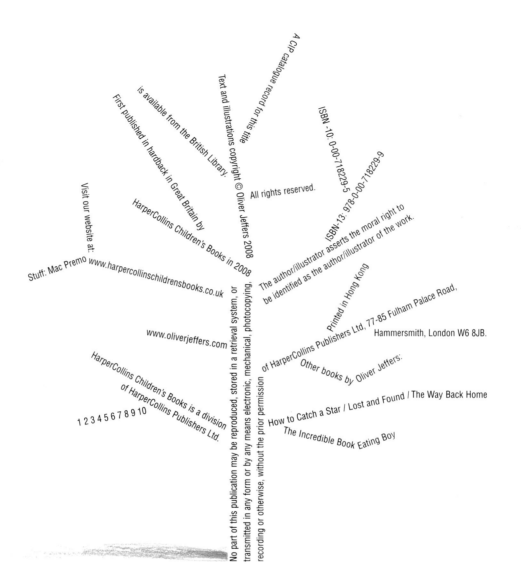

A CIP catalogue record for this title

Text and illustrations copyright © Oliver Jeffers 2008

is available from the British Library.

First published in hardback in Great Britain by

HarperCollins Children's Books in 2008

ISBN -10: 0-00-718229-5

ISBN-13: 978-0-00-718229-9

The author/illustrator asserts the moral right to
be identified as the author/illustrator of the work.

Visit our website at:

Stuff: Mac Premo www.harpercollinschildrensbooks.co.uk

Printed in Hong Kong

of HarperCollins Publishers Ltd, 77-85 Fulham Palace Road,

Hammersmith, London W6 8JB.

www.oliverjeffers.com

Other books by Oliver Jeffers:

HarperCollins Children's Books is a division
of HarperCollins Publishers Ltd.

How to Catch a Star / Lost and Found / The Way Back Home

1 2 3 4 5 6 7 8 9 10

The Incredible Book Eating Boy

for Cate

Mixed Sources
Product group from well-managed
forests and other controlled sources
www.fsc.org Cert no. SW-COC-1806
© 1996 Forest Stewardship Council
FSC

FSC is a non-profit international organisation established to promote the
responsible management of the world's forests. Products carrying the FSC
label are independently certified to assure consumers that they come
from forests that are managed to meet the social, economic and
ecological needs of present and future generations.

Find out more about HarperCollins and the environment at
www.harpercollins.co.uk/green

the

GREAT

PAPER CAPER

OLIVER JEFFERS

HarperCollins *Children's Books*

There was a time in the forest...

when everything was not as it should have been.

Everyone who lived there had been noticing strange things.
Branches, they agreed, should not disappear from trees like that.

Someone, they agreed again, must be stealing them
and they each in turn blamed the other.

But they all had a solid alibi which meant it couldn't possibly be them.
So the tree thief must be someone else.

It was all very
mysterious indeed.

An investigation was launched
to get to the bottom of things.

They were each given a different job to do so the tree thief could be caught.

They took photographs,
made notes and
examined every leaf.

But no matter how
hard they investigated,

no clues could be found.

Then an eyewitness report led them to some
evidence that had blown in not far away

and it had the bear's
paw prints all over it.

They had found their culprit.

The bear was brought in to have his picture taken

and was kept late into the night to answer questions.

The next day he confessed everything in court...

all about the paper airplane competition and how badly
he wanted to win, and he knew he wasn't very good,
and he had run out of paper, and he had no one to ask
for help. He was so sorry for taking their trees without
asking, he hadn't meant to do so much harm.

Hmm, well all right, they all thought.

But he'd have to make it up to them by replacing the trees.

And a paper plane competition indeed? That sounded interesting.

The bear kept his word

and made it up to them.

And as the others
helped him gather up
the old paper planes,
they had an idea...

they put them all together and made a new one.

fin

advanced paper PLANERY

MODEL № 38

the MIGHTY CONDOR

A GRACEFUL and intimidating aircraft that will cut the air like BUTTER.

STEPS

1. USE any piece of paper that has 4 sides

2. DO all the folds and things

3. the COMPLICATED bit

4. um... the MORE complicated bit.

5. Examine.

6. How it's supposed to look. Repeat if necessary.

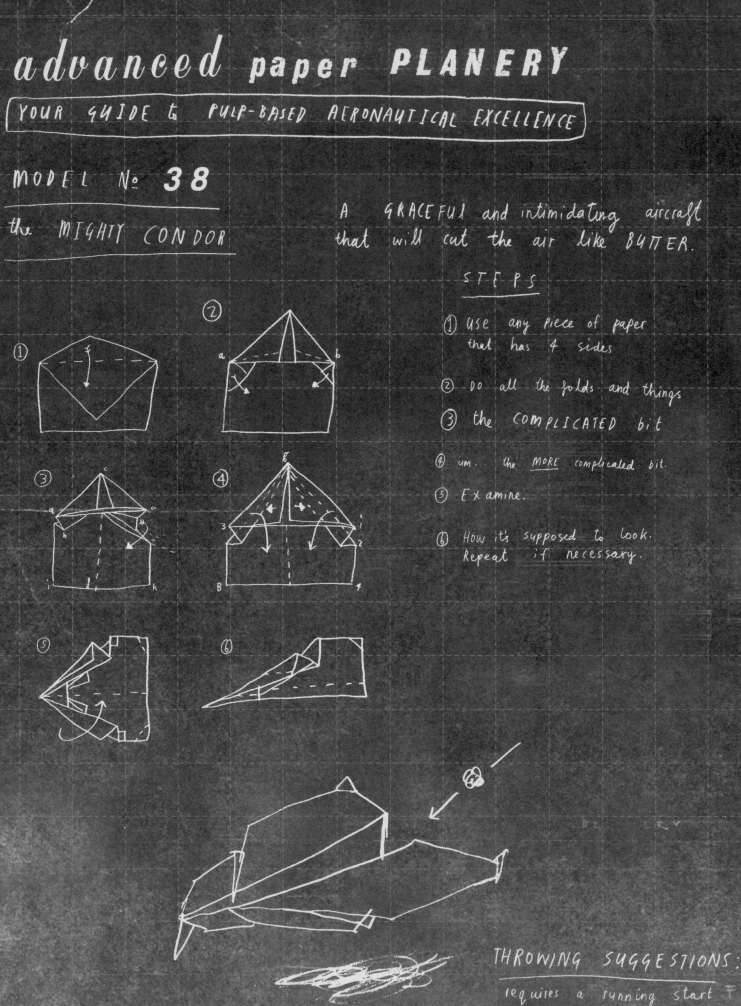

THROWING SUGGESTIONS:

requires a running start